P9-DYY-570

HIDDEN ROOTS

HIDDEN ROOTS

JOSEPH BRUCHAC

SCHOLASTIC PRESS
NEW YORK

LIBRARY OF CONGRESS CATALOGING-IN-PUBLICATION DATA
Bruchac, Joseph, 1942– • Hidden roots / by Joseph Bruchac. — 1st ed. p. cm.
Summary: Although he is uncertain why his father is so angry and what secret his mother is keeping from him, eleven-year-old Sonny knows that he is different from his classmates in their small New York town. [1. Family life — New York (State) — Fiction. 2. Indians of North America — New York (State) — Fiction. 3. Prejudice — Fiction. 4. New York (State) — Fiction.] I. Title.
PZ7.B82816Hi 2004   [Fic] — dc21   2003050396   ISBN 0-439-35358-0

10 9 8 7 6 5 4 3 2 1   04 05 06 07 08

Printed in the U. S. A.   37
First edition, February 2004
The text type was set in Sabon.
Book design by David Caplan

FOR ALL
   THOSE WHOSE
      NAMES ARE LOST

1954
AUGUST

MOON OF RIPENING

FLYING

I dug my paddle deeper. Just as I had expected, the prow of the canoe lifted up out of the water. We were rising above the lake. Its waters were now far below us. The tall pine trees on the shore looked as small as twigs. We were heading toward the sunrise, toward the top of the great mountain, paddling our canoe through the sky!

I wasn't alone in that canoe. Someone I couldn't see was there behind me, paddling and singing. It was the singing that was lifting us up into the clouds. I knew that voice, or at least I thought I did.

A hand grasped my shoulder and shook me gently. The canoe and the lake, the singing and the mountain, were gone. I opened my eyes just the tiniest crack. I was in my own little room, on the army cot that had been my bed since I was old enough to be taken out of the crib. I knew it had to be way before dawn; not even the smallest gleam of light was coming in through my window. I could barely make out the shadowy shape bent over me, but I could see enough to know, to my relief, for certain sure who it was.

I was surprised, though, that my mother had been able to come into my room without waking me up. I was a light sleeper. I'd been taught that it was good to not sleep too heavily. Otherwise you might get "crept up on." My mother had told me that for as long as I could remember. It wasn't the kind of reassuring thing that most kids would expect a mother to say. Most mothers tell their children that everything is going to be all right, no matter what. But most mothers weren't like mine.

⚬ ⚬ ⚬

I'd always known Mom was different from the other mothers. For one thing, she didn't come to school like a lot of mothers did, helping out the teacher or bringing cupcakes for birthday parties. All I ever brought in for class parties were paper napkins. Because my father worked at the paper mill, we never had any shortage of them.

I would have liked Mom to come to school, but there were times when she couldn't because her face was bruised or she had a black eye. When I was little I thought it was because she was clumsy and ran into things — that's what she told me. But even those few times when my mother did come to school, the other mothers laughed more than Mom. They talked louder. They baked and helped with book drives and did arts and crafts. I wasn't the only one who noticed. The other kids in my class did, too.

"My momma is always baking cookies for the class. What's the matter with your mother, Howie?" Verney Wooley was the first one I remember saying that. Even when we were in third grade he was already a head taller than me. He loomed over me on the playground like

Goliath glaring down at David. I should have just walked away and kept my mouth shut. But I didn't.

"There's nothing wrong with my mom," I said.

"You calling me a liar, Camp? Eh?" Verney said. I knew I was in trouble. Whenever Verney called anyone by their last name, the next thing was never pleasant. Sure enough, he pushed me hard in the chest, and I stumbled back.

The other kids on the playground had already formed a circle around us.

"Fight, fight, fight!" somebody was calling in an excited voice that was half yell and half whisper — loud enough for kids to hear but not loud enough to attract the attention of any teachers. I looked around the circle, hoping I'd see a friendly face. But all the eyes fixed on me looked mean. They wanted me to fight. I'd seen it happen before. All the other boys who were friends with Verney had fought him and lost and had then been accepted into his gang. I wasn't so sure I wanted that. Part of me was scared. But part of me was stubborn. They all wanted me to fight, so I wasn't going to give them that satisfaction. I turned around and began to push my way out of the crowd.

"Come back and fight. What are you, yellow? Eh?"

A hand swatted me in the back of the head so hard that it made me bite my tongue. But I didn't turn around, even when the chanting started. The fact that one of the girls started it made it even worse. I recognized her voice. It was Wendy Point, and I had a crush on her. Just that morning she'd smiled at me when she needed a pencil, and I had given her a new one from my pencil box.

"Howard's a coward, Howard's a coward."

I knew I was and that none of the kids would ever forget it. I knew that just as surely as I knew that I'd be in the same class in the Sparta Elementary School with those same mean kids for the rest of my life, and no one my age would ever like me.

I hunched my shoulders and headed for the door where the two teachers had been too busy smoking cigarettes to even notice what had happened. None of the other kids followed me, and I spent the rest of that recess alone in the classroom at my desk, writing my name on a piece of paper and then drawing a circle around it and then drawing an arrow through it.

I didn't tell my mother about what Verney said or about the kids all calling me Howard the Coward. There are some things you just never tell your mother. But I asked her why she was always telling me how important it was to watch my back and keep quiet and not get crept up on.

"Why aren't you like the other mothers?" My voice was angry, even though I didn't mean it to be. Once I got older, I realized I wasn't being fair. But Mom didn't get angry back at me. There was enough anger in our house without her adding to it.

"Maybe those mothers haven't lived through the 'no-matter-what' like I have," she said. She wouldn't tell me then what the "no-matter-what" was. I wasn't ready for it yet, she said, in a voice that was surprisingly soft. Then she wrapped her right hand around her left wrist, covering up the redness there that would later turn into a bruise.

⑥ ⑥ ⑥

The thought of being crept up on always scared me. When I was little, I wondered who was going to creep up on me. I'd seen a serial at the community theater where the cowboys had been attacked while they were sleeping, so my first question was natural.

"Will I be crept up on by Indians?" I asked.

"No," Mom said. Her voice became a little sad. "Not by Indians. Just crept up on. That's all."

The way she said "that's all" told me that I was done with asking questions. For then, at least.

So I practiced sleeping light, listening even when I was dreaming. I think that is when I started to dream in a different way. I think that was when I started hearing the songs in my dreams, when I started having new dreams. Dreams of climbing mountains that rose higher than any of those I saw in the light of day. Dreams of flying high over our little farm just outside of Sparta.

Even though we called our home "the farm," we really didn't farm it like some of the other families nearby did. The farm used to be a real farm once, but those days were gone. The only planting we did was Mom's vegetable garden out back. When she worked the soil, her hands seemed as gentle as when she brushed down the cowlick of hair on the back of my head. But even on that small plot of dirt, somehow Mom always managed to grow enough beans and corn, cucumbers and squash, tomatoes and peppers, beets and potatoes for our meals, with enough to spare for canning. The barn where there had once been cows had fallen down before I was born. Being so close to the Hudson River, the soil was good, even if it was rocky. But the fields where past generations had done haying and raised corn had grown up with sumacs and fire cherry, except for two acres that had been planted with Scotch pine for Christmas trees that still had to grow another three years before any of them could be harvested. I think that my father would have enjoyed just being a farmer. The rare times his shift at the mill allowed it, he helped Mom with the gardening. They smiled at each other more when they were in the garden, and I loved to run back and forth between them, helping out. But there was no real money in farming. And, besides that, with mill work, there was no time, especially when Daddy came home so late so many nights. Late and angry.

That August morning, even though I'd been crept up on, I didn't jump up or try to struggle. I had recognized that gentle touch on my shoulder. I knew whose voice I was about to hear.

"Sonny," Mom whispered. "Get up now, baby. Uncle Louis is coming to take us to see the deer."

I rolled over and opened my eyes all the way. "Is it safe?" I asked in a voice as soft as Mom's.

"It's safe," she said. "Daddy went off to the mill an hour ago."

My father had always worked at the mill. The hours were long, and the big machines that ran night and day making paper frightened me. The way they roared and clanked and then made sounds like giants trying to whisper. It seemed to me those machines were saying something.

Come too close to me and I'll get you.

It wasn't just my imagination, which was, I admit, wild enough on its own. My father told me as much the one time I went on a plant tour on Family Day. That was when they gave away things like little pads of paper to the kids and bundles of scratchy paper napkins to the mothers. We always had lots of those scratchy paper napkins on the dinner table — in part because no one ever really wanted to use them. But Daddy, who believed in saving whenever we could, would never allow my mother to buy cloth napkins or even paper ones that were softer than the sandpapery freebies. "Penny saved is a penny earned," he'd say. Every other month, the unused napkins, dusty and fading, would vanish to be replaced by new ones with a different pattern — HAPPY BIRTHDAY exchanged for TRIANGLE DINER.

"You don't want to get too close to Number Three there," Daddy said, pushing me toward a gray metal monster with a blanketed rolling pad that looked like a tongue stuck out at us. "That's the one took off Bill Ricker's arm to the elbow. And last year we had to shut it down and lose half a day's work just to get what was left of the Miller kid out of it."

Daddy's voice was hard, the way it got when he was angry. He'd seemed angry ever since we'd arrived for

Family Day, as angry as he got when he and Mom talked about the secret things in whispers so that I couldn't make out what they were saying. When he wasn't angry and he wasn't too tired from work, my father was gentle with me, played pitch and catch, or even took me fishing if it was a weekend he had off. I knew down deep that he loved me, but I also knew that when the anger was in him, it was safest for me to be someplace else.

I tried to pull back, but Daddy held on to both of my shoulders as he walked me even closer to the hungry-looking machine that reared up above me as tall as a hill. The fingers of his right hand dug deep into my shoulder and tears came to my eyes.

"No," I said in a small voice. I wanted to yell and struggle and try to get away, but knew that if I did he'd squeeze so hard I'd have bruises.

Mom reached out and pulled me away from him. I wanted to wrap my arms around her legs the way I used to do when I was little, but I knew Daddy would never stand for that.

"Jake!" she said to my father, her voice an angry whisper. "You're scaring him."

"Darn straight," Daddy said. "Only way to learn. He's only a kid now, but next thing you know he'll be out of high school and into the world. Hell, I never even got to go to high school." A muscle twitched in my father's jaw. "Whether he likes it or not. This way, when the time comes that he's working here he'll be that much more ready. Not like those green half-Indian kids who come out of those hills from up around Sacandaga and stick their fingers into the gears the first day they're here. Can't make a silk purse out of a sow's ear."

Mom didn't say anything to that. But I saw by the set of her mouth that there was something she wanted to say. As for me, I kept quiet while making myself a solemn vow, a promise of the sort that Uncle Louis had taught me to save in my heart and then speak aloud in the forest with some old cedar tree as a witness.

I will never as long as I live work in the mill.

I won't be one of those turning what's wild and free into napkins and toilet paper.

I will never be as angry as my father.

WORDS

It was 4:00 A.M. as I got dressed and then, still half asleep, tried to spoon the breakfast cereal into my mouth. I don't know what kind of cereal it was. It wasn't Wheaties or Cheerios. It was just the cheapest cereal on the shelf, the one we could afford. I thought how lucky it was that Daddy had an extra shift and had to go to work so early. Aside from the fact that, as always, we needed the money, Daddy not being here meant he couldn't tell us not to go with Uncle Louis.

It wasn't that Daddy disliked Uncle Louis. I'd overheard Daddy say to Mom that he liked him. Even respected him. Considering who he was, a French-Canadian and all, Daddy said, Uncle Louis had made something of himself. In the minds of some folks in the north country of New York State, French-Canadians weren't worth much. Uncle Louis, though, had a reputation as a trustworthy and hardworking hired man. He was also a hunter and a trapper, and was regarded by most as the best in the county. People respected a man who could hunt and trap, and that had especially been so back when Uncle Louis first moved into the town. That was in the 1930s when the game became scarce after they put in the big reservoir and flooded out the Sacandaga Valley. During the Depression — which was something bad that happened before I was born and might just happen again — Uncle Louis's trapping had been very important. Muskrat was good to eat and the pelts might bring in as much as fifty cents each. And later, when the young men were gone during the second world war, Uncle Louis had kept on hunting and trapping and fishing. He had provided for a lot of people, not just those he called nephew or niece, which was what he called Mom.

Uncle Louis, my mother had explained, wasn't really my uncle. He'd come to work for Mom's parents, Grama and Grampa John Henry, as a part-time hired man when she was a little girl. I don't have much memory of Grama Mary and Grampa John Henry. They passed on when I was three. From things Mom and Daddy sometimes said, not to me, things I overheard, I got the impression that I had some distant cousins somewhere. But if I did, I'd never met them. Mom had lost a child before me and another one after I was born, and now she couldn't have any other kids. I was an only child. I know she was sad about that, and I wonder if that wasn't why Daddy was disappointed in me sometimes. It isn't easy for one kid to be all the children his family will ever have. Since Daddy's parents had died of influenza when he was twelve, and Mom's parents passed on when I was three, Uncle Louis sort of filled in the place for me where most other kids had grandparents.

Still, Daddy and Uncle Louis didn't quite get along. I

wondered if Daddy resented Uncle Louis because Mom liked him so much. When they were together you could see that there was something special between them. Uncle Louis could just nod his head at my mother, and she would get this smile on her face as big as if he'd just praised her up one side and down the other. Which I suppose, in his quiet way, he had done. And Uncle Louis had this way of saying just a word or two or making a face when he said something that was just so funny you had to laugh. At least Mom and I did. Daddy rarely laughed and never made anyone else laugh, either.

The problem with Uncle Louis, I overheard Daddy say to Mom, was that he was going to fill my head with what Daddy called foolish notions. I had no idea what Daddy meant by that. Uncle Louis had never told me to do anything that didn't make perfect sense to me. Calling my attention to the way the geese talk to one another when they cross the sky, making certain I knew the difference between a squirrel track and the footprints of a rabbit in the snow, helping me understand how important it was to be quiet when you were out in the woods, to use your ears when most folks are flapping their jaws — those weren't foolish things at all. Of course, I never said so out loud to Daddy. But I think he could sense the way I listened up to Uncle Louis and even copied the way he walked, a careful, slow stride that hardly rustled the leaves when he was in the woods. So Daddy could not abide him coming around and talking to me when my father wasn't around. Otherwise, we might get into things I shouldn't hear about. There were just some things I was too young to understand.

For instance, I had already been told I was too young to understand why Uncle Louis didn't have children of his own.

"Hush up," Mom had snapped when I'd asked. Her stern tone surprised me. "You're too young to understand. That's all."

And that was the first and only time I ever asked about Uncle Louis's past, though it was far from the end of my wondering even more about it.

⚬   ⚬   ⚬

Uncle Louis was only one of the things not to be talked about when Daddy was around. Another was the second world war. Miss Anderson, my fifth-grade teacher, had brought up the war in school last spring.

"Some of your own parents served in the armed forces, boys and girls," she said. I remember how serious her voice had then become. "Some of them made the greatest sacrifice. Some were heroes."

She looked right at me and then smiled when she said that. Other kids noticed.

"Was your father a hero in the war? Eh?" Verney Wooley asked me as we waited in front of the school for our bus. I hadn't been able to answer him. So he punched me in the arm.

But when I got home, I asked the question as the three of us sat together for dinner.

"Were you a hero in the war, Daddy?"

There was a long silence. Mom picked up a paper napkin and began twisting it, the letters of EAT AT AL'S disappearing one by one as the napkin turned into shreds.

Then Daddy's voice came out, hard and slow, the way it always got when he was angry, and I knew I was in trouble, even if I didn't know why. His eyes narrowed and the big muscles of his jaw bulged. "Someone put you up to asking that, Sonny."

"Miss Anderson was talking about the war in school today," I said. I could feel my eyes getting moist. "She said some of our parents were heroes. That's all. Honest, Daddy." By now I was really crying. I didn't understand why. No more than I understood why Mom's eyes were full of tears, too.

Daddy got real quiet. He held up his hands and looked at them as if they belonged to somebody else. Then he folded his own paper napkin up into a small square and placed it on the table in front of him. He got up slowly from the table, scraping his chair back over the threadbare rug and the linoleum on the floor. He walked out of the room. We heard our front door open and close and then the sound of the Studebaker's starter whirring. The heavy tires grated over the gravel as Daddy backed the old car out of the driveway. Then he was gone.

Mom and I knew where he was going. When Daddy got quiet like that, there was only one place he went. I knew because I had followed him once after watching his car go down the street a quarter of a mile. That time he had paused for a long time at the stop sign, as if trying to decide which way to go — right onto the state road or straight ahead. But he had turned left over the railroad tracks, down to the park by the river behind the mill. There was a place where he sat on top of the cliffs where you could look down at the rushing water below the dam. He'd sit there for a long time. Then he'd come home and none of us would ever say a word about it.

I once asked Mom why he went there. Her tone told me she'd answer once — and only once. "The thing is, your daddy, he doesn't go out and drink like some do. And he always comes home. No matter what."

I knew I wasn't ever supposed to ask why my father got angry, but I had to know what had happened that day. I looked out the door, making sure that Daddy was really gone, that his car wasn't coming back. Even then I whispered when I said to my mother, "Why did Daddy get so angry at me when I asked him about the war?"

My mother looked at me. I could tell she knew the answer but wasn't certain she should say.

"Please tell me," I said, "I didn't mean to be bad."

My mother pressed her apron to her face and then reached out her hand to grasp my shoulder. "Sonny, you weren't bad," she said. "You weren't." She took a deep breath and looked toward the door. Then she looked back at me and this expression came over her face. It was a look of quiet determination that I hadn't seen there before, even though I knew it reminded me of someone else. I wasn't sure who.

"It's time I told you," she said, "about Daddy and the war. After his parents died, and the bank took their house, he left school and earned his keep as a hired boy at one farm or another until he was finally old enough to get a job in the mill. Your daddy was my boyfriend by then, and we were planning to get married when he had enough saved up. Then the war started, and your father decided that he had to enlist. I told him I didn't want him to go, but he said that he had to do it. He said it was his only chance to prove to people around here that he amounted to something. He'd be seen as a hero and not just a poor orphan boy with no education. So he quit his job at the mill and joined the Marines.

"The week before he was supposed to ship out, he came home on leave. He looked so handsome in his uniform that people really were impressed. But the day before he was to go overseas, something happened."

My mother took a deep breath and looked at the door again.

"It's all right," I whispered, "I've been listening for the car. Daddy's still gone."

Mom nodded, bit her lip, and then continued. "Tom Miller, one of the men who worked with your father at the mill, had gotten a motorcycle, a shiny new Indian. Tom had never treated your father with any respect before, but now that he was a Marine it was different. He asked your father if he'd like to take a ride on the Indian."

Mom breathed in again and closed her eyes. It was as if she were seeing that day all over again. She shook her head and then wiped her face again with her apron. "Daddy lost control of that big motorcycle when he was going over the railroad tracks by the cemetery. He was thrown right over the cemetery wall and his head struck hard against a gravestone. He had a bad concussion.

When he came to, he'd been in a coma for ten days. His unit had shipped out without him."

Because my father had been hurt so badly, the doctor told him he couldn't be a soldier. He was given a medical discharge. He and Mom got married two months later. After a while, even though he felt ashamed to go back there, he got back his job at the mill. He needed it because Mom said they were starting a family. He also did volunteer work, taking care of war supplies, in a warehouse in Glens Falls to help the war effort. He joined the Civil Defense, too, and was made a warden, doing things like watching out for enemy aircraft. There wasn't really much chance the Germans were ever going to attack Sparta, but Daddy was proud to be a warden, even though some mean-spirited people made fun of the Civil Defense.

Mom said he'd been lucky, not just surviving the accident, but also not going overseas. Half the men in his unit never came home again. They ended up buried under foreign gravestones in Normandy. But Daddy didn't feel that he'd been lucky. She said he had headaches a lot now, and he got angry quicker than before. A big part of him felt bad about the fact that men he'd been friends with had been killed in the fighting while he was safe at home. He thought people looked at him funny because of that, added on to the fact that he'd been a poor, uneducated orphan to begin with. The war hadn't made things better for him at all. That was why he would never talk about it, why Mom could never mention the war in front of him.

And now, I too, had more words I couldn't say, more things not to be talked about.

LOUIS

There are few times as quiet as the last hours before dawn. Because it was late August, three months past the time of the blackflies and a month or more before the first real frost, all our windows were open, even the ones that had no screens on them.

A mosquito might still get in, but it was worth the price of a bite to have the fresh air, Mom always said.

So, with those open windows, it was easy to hear

what sounded like the call of a loon drifting inside our house.

"Uncle Louis!" I said, jumping up from the table.

Before I could reach the front door, Mom had opened it. Uncle Louis stood there, looking like he always did. He was wearing his old red wool coat and a tattered green guide's hat with fishing flies, which he had tied himself, stuck in the red band that circled it. His white hair was longer than most men wore it, almost down to his shoulders. His face was tanned darker, too, than the faces of most of the people in our town. I'd noticed that in the summer I got almost as dark as Uncle Louis except his color didn't fade in the winter. And, whereas my own eyes were a sort of greenish brown, his eyes, which were squintier than mine, were as black as a night with no moon or stars. Although Uncle Louis was said to be French-Canadian, he never wore a mustache like a lot of French-Canadian men did. His face was clean shaven and, as always, there was a little smile on his lips.

He patted his chest with his left hand and then placed that hand on Mom's right shoulder. It was the way he always greeted her when Daddy wasn't around. Mom pursed her lips up a little, like she was about to say something, or else trying not to. Then she did the same as Uncle Louis, hand to heart, shoulder touch. It happened fast, so fast that it took me some years to notice how they always did that. But now that I was eleven and going to be in sixth grade, I was noticing most things, or so I thought.

Then Uncle Louis held out his arms to me. I ran right over and hugged him. It wasn't a little-kid hug. Uncle Louis had made that clear to me. It was a hug between two men. It ended with us slapping each other on the back with both palms and then stepping back. It had been almost three months since I'd seen Uncle Louis, and I could feel him sizing me up, so I stood up a little on my toes.

"Growing," Uncle Louis said, approval in his voice.

"Two inches taller since April," I said.

"Sonny," Mom said. She never let me get away with exaggeration.

"Well, an inch at least," I said.

"Tall enough to see the mountaintop," Uncle Louis said. I wasn't quite sure what that meant, but I liked the sound of it.

"Tall enough to see the mountaintop," I repeated.

Uncle Louis pointed toward the open door behind him with his thumb and raised one white eyebrow. I understood the question.

"We're ready to go see the deer," I said.

VERMONT

Vermont. Most people hearing that name just think of the state. But for me it was always something different. Even though I could see the tops of its mountains to the east of our Adirondack hills, Vermont seemed to be so strange and far away, a place with something about it that was mysterious and maybe even a little threatening. Uncle Louis had lived there once, but bad things had happened, and he had vowed to never live there again. I wasn't quite sure what those things were, but from what I'd overheard, it had something to do with Indians.

I didn't know much about Indians, except what I heard in school or saw in the movies. I knew they were mostly all gone, dead, or had run off to the West. Real Indians, I mean, who rode horses and hunted buffalo and all of that. People in Sparta talked about those dirt-poor half-Indian families that lived up on the other side of the mountain, but they weren't real Indians from what I heard. They lived in shacks, not tepees, and they didn't ride horses; they rode around in old jalopies. They didn't even wear feathers. I was told they had a lot of kids, but I never met any of them because they went to school in Hadley.

I'd heard how the forests were wilder in parts of Vermont than they were here in our Adirondack Mountains. It made me think that maybe some real Indians had been able to hide out in those Vermont forests. The movies had taught me that real Indians could be dangerous. So they were likely the ones who had done the bad things that made Uncle Louis leave. But I'd never been to Vermont or talked to anyone who had been there other than Uncle Louis, so I couldn't say for sure. Mom told me that we still had some distant relatives in Vermont, but I'd never met them. I assumed that was because they didn't like us.

I was excited that morning, as we drove toward the dawn. Uncle Louis was behind the wheel of his old blue Plymouth, and I was right next to him. Mom had asked me if I wanted to sit by the window, but I preferred the middle. I could pretend that I was driving. If I was real good, Uncle Louis might even let me hold the wheel with him like he had done a time or two before.

As we rolled along, we sometimes went as much as fifty miles an hour. That was fast for two-lane roads with spots that were still just stone and gravel and not paved at all. None of us said anything and that was fine. There seemed to be as much said by Uncle Louis's silence as there were in the words others spoke. It was comfortable — comfortable as the smell of cedar and smoke that was as much a part of him as that green guide's hat or his moccasins.

The sky ahead was getting a little lighter as we went through the town of Arlington. The mountains were close to the road here, leaning over us like friendly giants. It seemed at times as if Uncle Louis could hear my thoughts, and this was one of those times.

"You like those mountains?" he asked, pointing up with his chin. He never pointed with his finger. To do that was rude. I tried to remember to always point with a turn of my head or with my lips like he did, but it wasn't easy.

I nodded my head.

"Good," Uncle Louis said. "Those mountains like us, too. You don't never have to be afraid of the mountains. It's just some of the people that you have to watch out for."

We were out of the town now and back in the countryside. The hills rolled down to the road, and there were no other cars in sight. Uncle Louis switched off the headlights, turned off the key, put the car into neutral, and let it glide forward another hundred yards before pulling off the road.

With the headlights off, you could see that dawn was almost here. It was all red above the hills in front of us. Uncle Louis placed two fingers on his lips. I nodded again. I knew it meant to be dead quiet. Then he rolled down his window and leaned out, making room for me to lean out right next to him. On the other side of the car, Mom had rolled down her window, too.

Together, we looked into the darkness. There were shapes out there that were moving. I remember thinking they might be cows and that we were looking up into some farmer's hillside pasture. Then the darkness began to melt away. Slowly at first, and then, as the sun cleared the hilltop, quicker than a thought, the shadows went running away toward the west. Birds had already been chirping, even before dawn, but now they were flying up from the hills to sing their greetings to the new day. But it was not the birds that I saw most clearly that dawn. It was the dark, slow-moving shapes that I had barely been able to make out when I first saw them. Deer. Some were so close to the car I could almost reach out and touch them. They were all over the hillside, a whole herd of them.

As we watched, I suddenly realized that the door was moving. Uncle Louis must have popped the latch even before we had pulled off the road. He slowly pushed the door open, no more than an inch at a time, his hand on my shoulder to steady me. His feet were in the grass and now mine were, too.

"Let us go say hello," he whispered.

Then, moving with slow careful steps, my left hand in his, my other hand held out in greeting, Uncle Louis and I walked among the deer. Heads raised to look at us, tails switched back and forth as we passed them, but not one of them ran away.

"Hello," I whispered to each of them as we walked slowly past.

We made a slow circle, reaching the car just as a big new Buick came around the corner. It squealed to a stop and a man thrust his arm out the window.

"Holy cow!" the man yelled. "Will you look at that?"

There was not much to look at. As soon as his car had stopped, every deer in the field had taken flight. In no more time than it took to take two deep breaths, they were gone from sight. But not from my memory.

"Time to go home," Mom said.

HiDING

As we drove home from Vermont that morning, Uncle Louis talked to me about the way deer keep themselves from being seen. He explained how a deer can move through the forest quieter than a little squirrel.

"I've sat up on a hill," he said, "and watched half a dozen deer down below work their way 'round a bunch of hunters. Not one of them men ever knowed a deer was there."

We stopped at a place that sold maple sugar candy. It was one of my mother's favorite things, and it wasn't too expensive. Uncle Louis insisted on buying a whole box, with each candy in a little red folded paper cup.

Each piece of candy was in the shape of a maple leaf and there were a dozen of them. Even though maple sugar candy was my mother's favorite, I have to admit that I ended up with seven pieces while she had only four. The first one was for Uncle Louis, who would accept no more than that. There was no point bringing any back to Daddy. He didn't much like sweet things. And this was meant to be a secret trip. I wasn't sure that I felt good about keeping secrets from Daddy this way. But I knew, as did Mom and Uncle Louis, that it would be best if we kept the trip to Vermont from my father.

Uncle Louis took as long to eat one piece of candy as it took me to eat seven. Then he smiled at me, and I could tell he was about to continue the conversation we'd been having before we'd stopped for the deer — even though it had been at least an hour ago.

Talking with Uncle Louis was like that. He might start telling me something one day but not finish it off.

"We'll tie a knot in it here," he'd say, and then leave. Even if a month went by before I saw him again, he'd pick it right up where he'd left off. It taught me things about both listening and remembering. Like what he said next.

"Sometimes," he said, "the only way to survive is to hide. The deer do it and we can do it, too. Even if we have to do it in plain sight."

I didn't quite understand that, but I trusted that if I kept it in my memory, the understanding would come to me sooner or later. But there was no time to think more about it that day. For when we pulled the car down the lane toward our house, we saw exactly what my mother and I had hoped we would not see.

My father was home. He was sitting on the front steps, holding his billed cap in his hand. He looked angry.

HEARTBEAT

Although my father's face looked angry, and my mother looked worried as we pulled in, the look on Uncle Louis's face didn't change. There was no expression at all. Uncle Louis seemed as calm and peaceful as the surface of the river above the power dam.

My father stood up, but didn't walk toward the car. He just waited as the three of us walked over to him. It was only fifty feet, but it seemed like a hundred miles to me. Mom's hands were on my shoulders, or I wouldn't have been able to make my feet move.

In the time that it took us to cross the space between the car and the front steps where my father stood, it felt as if a thousand thoughts ran through my mind. When my father was really angry, he seemed to be capable of anything. Not just "giving me a swat" as he put it, but exploding into a rage so powerful that I was sure it could bring down the house. But when we reached him, my father didn't move his hands, not at first. He said a word. It was one that I'd heard some of the older kids who hung out by the drugstore say. But I'd never heard him say it before. It was a bad word, I knew, but it sounded ten times worse when he said it. The older kids were just trying it out. From my father's mouth it was as painful as a blow.

"I didn't know you'd be home," my mother said, her grip tightening on my shoulder.

"I know," said my father. Then he laughed, but it wasn't like he was laughing at something funny. "They changed my shift. They can do whatever they want with us. You ought to know that by now."

"Jake," Mom said. Just that, nothing more. But the word was a whole lot of things rolled up into one. It was an apology, a question, and, in some strange way, a kind of defiance.

"I told you, Martha," my father said. His voice was tight, his words as short as knots. "I told you not to go no place with him. A man is known by the company he keeps."

"Jake, he's my . . ." my mother started to say. Then she caught herself, even before my father held up his hand, as if trying to catch her words and stop them like you might try to catch a spear thrown at you.

"Don't you ever say it," my father said, his voice sounding angry and scared at the same time. He took half a step forward and his right hand was trembling now. I knew he was going to hit someone. Usually there was just the one time, and then he'd be sorry. He'd be helping me or my mother up and saying he'd never do it again. If I could just manage to get between him and my mother, it would be me. Mom tried to push me behind her, but I pulled free. I'd be the one who Daddy would be apologizing to and saying he didn't mean it and it would never happen again. Even though we all knew it would.

But before my father's hand could descend like a lightning bolt from the sky, Uncle Louis stepped forward. He did it so fast that I don't remember seeing him move. All I know is that one minute he was behind us on the other side of the car, and the next he was holding my father's right wrist in a grip so strong that even my father couldn't break free. Daddy was a head taller than Uncle Louis, but in that moment it seemed to me as if he were a child being held back from doing something foolish by a grown-up. At that moment, something seemed to change between all four of us, even though none of us quite knew what it was. Then Uncle Louis reached out and put his left hand on my father's chest.

"Jake," he said. "It don't matter whether she says it or not. We are who we are. It's you just as much as it is Martha or Sonny or me. You can't change that no more than you can change your own heartbeat."

Everything went silent. In that sudden quiet I could

swear I heard a drumbeat. It was pounding with a rhythm that seemed to weave my mom and Uncle Louis and me — and even Daddy — together. Then I realized it was the sound of my own heart.

A voice broke the rhythm. It was so small, so full of pain that it shocked me. It was my father's voice. "Lemme go," it said. "Please, Louis! Lemme go."

Uncle Louis stepped back from my father. Daddy looked at us as if he was about to say something. Then he bit his lip. He turned, walked to his car, climbed in, and drove away.

SEPTEMBER

MOON OF
LEAVES CHANGING

WOOD

The rest of that summer went by almost the way a log goes over the falls. It was there one minute, seeming as if it would float along forever, and then suddenly it was beyond the brink. The next time you saw it, it was far downriver in a swirl of water and then out of sight.

No one said anything to me about that morning my mother and Uncle Louis and I went to see the deer. No one explained why Daddy had been so upset or what it was that he feared. No one said why we shouldn't spend time with Uncle Louis. And no one spoke about how Uncle Louis kept my father from hitting — or how we went through the whole rest of the summer without my father ever once giving me a swat or raising his voice.

None of it was discussed, but I still wondered. There was so much to wonder about. Why was it that Daddy didn't want Uncle Louis around? What was it that Mom and Uncle Louis knew that scared Daddy? And why did it feel that as different as we were, we belonged together — all four of us? I wondered about a lot. But I didn't ask. I'd learned that not asking kept things more peaceful. I added it all to my growing list of things not to ask about — like Uncle Louis's past and the war.

Then my father came to me after breakfast on a late summer Saturday morning while my mother was out getting groceries at the store.

"I want to show you something, Howard," he said. He hardly ever used my given name. His voice was so quiet — not ordering me, but asking in a way he never had before — that when he held out his hand I took it.

It wasn't far from our house to the river. I was

surprised to find out that Daddy knew the same secret trail to get there that I thought only I knew. At the end of the trail we could see down below the paper plant. I looked at the river, hoping I'd see it, even though it wasn't always there. But that day I was lucky.

"Look," I said, "the river is full of rainbows!"

My father let go of my hand and pushed his dark hair back from his forehead. "You could say that," he said.

And it was true. Just below the plant, in a spreading bright arc, the water of the upper Hudson was turning as many colors as you could ever imagine. Glowing greens, brilliant yellows, bright blues, and reds, even black. Above the plant the water was nothing but shades of blue. It was only below the outlet pipes that it got so pretty.

My father put his hand on my shoulder. "I want to tell you something, Howard," he said. "You ready to listen?"

That was a funny question, for listening was second nature to me by then. But my father, unlike Uncle Louis, would not accept silence as an answer.

"Are you?" he said.

"I'm ready to listen."

My father inhaled deeply, as if it would take a good

deal of breath to get out the words he had to say. "What looks pretty there in the water," he said, "really isn't pretty. The plant is dumping out the waste from making paper. There's something like oil in it and lots of other . . . chemicals. They hurt our river, son. They poison it, and they kill the fish. Someday we're all going to have to pay for what they're doing now."

"If it's bad, why are they doing it, Daddy?" I was confused. Until then I'd always assumed that anything that looked pretty was a good thing.

"Why do they do it?" my father said. Unlike Uncle Louis, Daddy didn't always seem certain of what he said, even though he used more words. My father always seemed to have to repeat the questions I asked him, as if he needed more time to think. He pushed his hair back from his forehead again and took another deep breath. "They do it because they can. Just because they can."

Then my father grabbed my shoulder and shook it so hard that it hurt some. "Remember that?" he said, his voice fierce.

"I will," I said.

And then I smiled a little, not on my face, but inside.

What my father had told me had made it clear to me that my decision to never work in the mill was a good one.

Not ever, I thought, *not ever!*

⑤　⑤　⑤

School would start soon. I had a theory that if I didn't notice it, it wouldn't notice me, either. For a while, it seemed to work. Keeping quiet and keeping my head down had kept me out of trouble. But I was going to start sixth grade now. I'd grown over the summer, but I doubted it was enough for the other kids to notice. The boys would surely still be bigger than me and even some of the girls were probably still taller than I was.

"The short trees grow faster," Uncle Louis said to me one day when he saw me sizing myself up in front of the mirror. "The big ones grow slower because they're putting down deeper roots."

Daddy was not around that day. Uncle Louis had taken to dropping by during the day, sometimes two or three times a week. Daddy wasn't around much at all, in fact. He was too busy at the mill — working double shifts now.

51

It wasn't just that he was living those words he always said to us — *Early to bed, early to rise, makes a man healthy, wealthy, and wise.* Even when he didn't have to be at work he had taken to walking out of the house. He seemed to do that every time he was about to lose his temper over something, times when, in the past, he would have yelled or hit someone.

My mother had twice as much to do herself around the house. It wasn't just her own work, but the man's-work chores that Daddy didn't have the time to do between shifts. I helped a lot. At least that's what Mom told me.

Before long, the days would be getting short and the leaves would turn red as bear blood. I held the ladder while Mom wrestled to get the heavy storm windows into place. It was also my job to latch the windows on the bottom while she turned the top wing nuts I couldn't reach.

I noticed that the pile of split wood for our stoves grew every time Uncle Louis came around. There were already two whole new cords of it, mostly seasoned ash. It was stacked up in the corner on the screen porch so the pieces could be handed in through the porch window. It was my job to fill the wood box. In the winter, nothing in the world is hungrier than a wood box. I sometimes suspected that wood box ate up the wood I put in it even before we got it into the woodstove oven in the kitchen.

Uncle Louis was better and faster with an ax than most men were with a chainsaw. Daddy had not been free to do the stacking and splitting. And, strong as she was, Mom was never good with an ax. But in Uncle Louis's hands, an ax would come alive, floating like a bird. Whether snicking the limbs off a felled log or splitting wood, Uncle Louis made it all seem effortless, as if the ax were doing the work. He'd worked, the big woods as a lumberman until he was in his sixties. That was ten years ago. Now his only woods work was providing a few cords for folks who didn't have the time to get their own. I don't think he ever accepted much money for it, saying it was just trash wood he'd picked up from the road's edge.

I spun the last latch tight and left Mom to finish the work of tightening the wing nuts.

"Can I help?" I asked Uncle Louis.

In answer, he began stacking wood in my arms. Dry,

end-checked maple this time. Uncle Louis's "trash wood" was always like that. Well-seasoned cherry, maple, or ash. The best burning wood you could imagine. I'd never been to his place, but I imagined that the wood piles behind it stretched for miles. I hoped that now that I was in sixth grade Uncle Louis would take me to see his cabin up on the mountain. For some reason, Mom insisted that it was better for me not to go there until I was older. I couldn't understand why that was so, but I accepted it as just another one of those things.

Uncle Louis was one of the men who'd been hired to clear away the trees when they put in the Sacandaga Reservoir. He'd worked in a clearing crew with men like Larry Older and Jess Bowman, who now ran the general store twelve miles down the road with his wife. But more than trees were cut out of the valley. Whole towns were moved, even their churches and cemeteries. Most didn't talk about it, but Uncle Louis said some of those in the valley who were forced out were men and women who had no paper title to their land, people living in the simplest way, in log cabins and little houses with shingles made of bark.

For some reason that lost valley, which was just over the hills a few miles from us, came to my mind that early autumn day.

"What was it like clearing trees for the reservoir?"

"Hard," he said. "But the wood work wasn't the hardest. The hardest was to clear away the houses and the shacks and the people who was in them."

The word "shacks" made me think of the poor half-Indians on the other side of our mountains. "Were they Indians?" I asked Uncle Louis.

"Some of them used to be," he said, turning his face toward the peaks rising to the north of town.

"What do you mean?" I said. I didn't understand how Indians could stop being Indians.

Uncle Louis reached out his left hand to take hold of my shoulder and gently pull me over to him so that we were both looking up at the range where a few maple trees had already turned crimson. "Because they was Indians," he said, raising his other hand as if he was greeting those mountains, "they got treated worse than everyone else. Some places, Indians been treated like they aren't even human. Or they'd say that all Indians was thieves and you could never trust them. Sometimes they'd have their land taken away from them, and they'd be made to move on, just because they was Indian. So some Indians just started telling people they weren't Indian, trying to live in ways that didn't seem to be the ways Indians lived. That way they'd be left alone — or so they thought."

I halfway understood. I felt sorry for those Indians, having to pretend like that. But I wondered why it was they thought they could fool people. Wouldn't you just have to look at them to see who they really were? I knew what Indians looked like from the movies. I'd seen how they danced and sang and played their drums. Or could Indians look and act like everybody else?

Before long, we'd finished unloading the truck. Another full cord of wood, four feet wide, four feet high, and eight feet long, sat next to the first two. It was enough to get us through the winter and more.

"You ever hear the bells?" Uncle Louis said.

I didn't know what he meant, but it seemed like "no" would be the right answer. So that was what I said.

"No."

Uncle Louis sat on the back of the empty truck bed, and I hopped up next to him.

"There's places," he said, "where you can stand by Old Sacandag on a quiet evening and listen. If a man has the patience to listen, he might hear those bells. Church bells coming from those little settlements that was there and now is under deep water."

Uncle Louis took off his hat to wipe his brow with his big red handkerchief.

"Listen long enough," he said, "and you might hear other things, too." He tapped his chest with his right palm, making a thumping sound.

"Like Indian drums?" I asked.

Uncle Louis smiled. "Maybe so."

"I'll listen," I said.

"I know you will," he answered. "I know you will."

THE LIBRARY

Fall was my favorite time of year. Everything seemed so clear and clean in the autumn light. You could see the top of Potash and the other mountains around us better than at any other season. And when you actually climbed one of those bare-top mountains, you could just about see forever from the peak. In the old days, the Indians who used to live here had climbed that mountain to greet the dawn and pray. I knew that because of Uncle Louis. The week before school began he had been telling me more about the Indians and their ways.

"There is where the old people would greet the dawn," he said, pointing with his chin to the top of Potash, a great big plug of stone, above the river and the hills. Then he looked back at me. "How early can you wake up, Sonny?"

"As early as you want, Uncle Louis."

I was wide awake and dressed at 5:00 A.M. when his truck pulled into the drive. Daddy was working the night shift, and Mom had seen no reason to tell him what I was doing. I walked out on quiet feet, remembering what Uncle Louis had told me the night before. "Not a word till we're ready to pray."

I must have fallen asleep in the truck because no sooner had I climbed in and shut the door and closed my eyes for just a second than I felt Uncle Louis's rough, cool hand on my forehead, and I opened my eyes and saw we were parked by the brook that flowed down from the mountain. It was so dark still that I shouldn't say that I saw the brook. I knew it was there because I heard it. And how beautiful a sound it was, that singing trickle of swift water over the stones. It was a sound you could never hear so clearly except when it was not yet day and even the birds had not begun to sing.

We didn't use any kind of light. Uncle Louis led the way, and I could just make out his dark outline ahead of me. I'd also learned that you can almost always see some light, even on the darkest night, by looking up to the sky and seeing the opening in the trees above a trail. I stumbled once or twice and hit my knee hard on a rock, but I didn't say a word. Being quiet like that made it so I could hear just about everything, from the sound of our breathing and the scuff of my soles on the hard stones, to the rattle and scurry of some little creature digging itself into the leaves by the trail.

We seemed to walk for hours, though I knew it couldn't have been that long because the sun had not yet risen. There was enough light for me to see how the exposed roots of the last big trees before the bare summit held to the mountain. Up so high and hard, roots can't dig in, but have to spread out. It was amazing to see how wide they reached, how much it takes to hold up a tree, how much is necessary that is hidden under the soil. We climbed on those bare roots, using them like steps, pulled ourselves onto the wide sloping ledge and made our way to the very top where there was a natural basin in the granite. The stars were starting to fade into the sky and the clouds to the east were starting to show that first color before the sun, a color like the petals of wild roses.

On the last part of our climb, I had been gathering dry branches in one arm like Uncle Louis had told me to do the night before. It had made the climbing a little harder, but I had a good stack of them of various sizes, from slender pine twigs up to firewood chunks of dry white birch tinder. When I put down what I had, I could see from the little smile on Uncle Louis's face that I'd done a good job.

He built a little tepee for the fire in almost no time with pine twigs and strips of birch bark in the heart and larger branches on the outside. There was an opening like a door, directly toward the east. Uncle Louis handed me his matches and held up his index finger. I understood. I could only use one match to light it.

I got down on my stomach with my arms in front of me and my face close to that opening. A gentle breeze had begun to blow, and I sheltered the matchbook with my cupped hands and my body. I lit it, flicking the match away from me so that it flared into flame right in the heart of the fire tepee where the dry birch caught quicker than paper. I didn't even have to blow on it. It caught so fast that it almost singed my eyebrows, and I had to lean back. The morning breeze made the fire burn stronger, so strong you could hear a sound like breathing as Uncle Louis's dark hands piled more wood onto it. He reached into his pocket, pulled out his pouch of Red Man tobacco, carefully folded it open, then looked at me and cupped his hand. I held my hand out and he dumped a handful of tobacco into it. Then he looked at the fire and spoke for the first time.

"We thank ye for your light and for keeping us good and warm," he said. Then he gave a little yell, almost like a fox's yelp, and opened his hand to drop his own handful of tobacco into the fire. He nodded at me, and I did the same. Then the two of us sat and faced the east and waited. A wave of birdsong was coming toward us from the direction of the sunrise, which was making the sky as red as the fire in front of our feet. It swept up the mountain until the birds were singing around us, sparrows and chickadees and more, waking up in the little bushes that grew around the edge of the mountaintop, like hair around the balding head of an old man.

Then the top edge of the sun was there, molten and glowing and breathing with life, just like our fire, and I could see it moving, lifting up into the sky. It was so breathtaking that it took me a moment to realize Uncle Louis was whispering something in my ear, "Remember, Sonny," he said. "Now don't you never forget it."

I nodded to him, knowing I didn't have to say anything.

"Isn't that something?" he whispered. "Funny how just about the only times of the day you ever really see the sun move is at the very start and near the very end. Just when it is beginning and just afore it is time to rest."

Uncle Louis stood up and I stood with him. He raised both his hands high over his head, and I did the same.

"We thank ye for giving us another day," he said to the sun.

"We thank ye for giving us another day," I said.

"Is it all right, us praying like Indians that way?" I asked Uncle Louis as we were climbing back down the mountain.

"Long as no one sees us," he said.

⑤ ⑤ ⑤

What spoiled the autumn some was going back to school. I still didn't really have any friends there. Sixth graders were not required to ride the bus if they didn't live too far out. School was close, only three-quarters of a mile away, so I walked. I always walked alone, and I hung back from the groups of kids I saw ahead of me. I'd learned not to give anyone a chance to notice me. So far, my strategy of keeping my head down and going along without being seen was working.

That was true in the classroom and on the playground. I did what I was told and spoke when I was spoken to. The rest of the time I just kept my head down. It had been that way ever since kindergarten. Even my teachers didn't pay me much attention. I wasn't a brain like Louise LaFavor, who never put her hand down in class and always did extra work. I wasn't good-looking and popular like Wendy Point or Andy Grander. I wasn't good at sports like Verney Wooley, who was always one of the captains whenever the boys got together to play basketball or touch football.

But I wasn't bullied much, especially since I had refused to fight. I just wasn't noticed. On the playground, I was usually the last one picked when they were choosing up sides for basketball or touch football or kickball. I wasn't that bad at sports, I just wasn't outstanding. I didn't try that hard and hung back as much as I could. It would have been worse to try real hard and make yourself noticed and then fail rather than just doing things halfheartedly or staying in the background. Whenever a basketball came into my hands, I would never shoot it, I'd just pass it to someone else, even if they were on the other team.

There was one thing, though, that I liked about school. I liked the books. We never had many of them in our house, and we really couldn't afford to buy more. The school had one whole room that was nothing but bookshelves and books. It wasn't as big a library as the one in our town, but it was better. The town library didn't have many books that were just for kids. That was all they had in the school library. Thanks to a grant from the mill, this was the first year in a long time there'd been more money in the school budget. Not only was the library being expanded, now we were even going to have our own librarian to shelve the books and do whatever else it was that a librarian did — though I wasn't quite sure what that was. Up till now, the work in the library had been done by Mr. Weble, the janitor. Maybe when she wasn't shelving books, the librarian's job would be to wash the windows and sweep the floor like he had done.

"I'm going to start reading here and not stop till I get all the way around the room," I said as I stood in the school library on the second day of school that autumn when more than just the leaves were changing.

I thought I was alone, but I wasn't.

"That is a noble ambition, young man," a voice said from behind me. Soft as it was, that voice shocked me. I turned around to see someone leaning over to look at me from the top of the big desk at the front of the room. I had the feeling that I might be in trouble. It was recess. I wasn't supposed to be in the library.

The person behind the desk stood up and came around. She was about the strangest adult I'd ever seen. She wasn't very tall. But her hair made up for her lack of height. It was yellow as an electric daisy and stood up like a beehive on her head.

The rest of that woman who was walking toward me was just as memorable as her hair. Her nose was long and sharp. She had huge wing-shaped black horn-rimmed glasses. They were so far down on the end of her nose they looked about ready to fall off. Likely they had done so in the past because she had a silver chain fastened to them that went around her neck. She had on rose-pink lipstick, kind of a dawn color, like my mom's. She wore a dress that was long and black and buttoned up to her neck. On her feet were white sneakers. PF-Flyers.

She held out her long right hand to me. That hand was the most unusual thing of all about her. First of all, it was big, as big as the hand of someone who might be twice her size. Then there were her fingernails. They had to be two-and-a-half inches long. And each one was painted a different color with a little picture in the middle. One painted nail had a pig on it, another had a beautiful black horse, another a collie dog, another a sailor with a parrot on his shoulder. On her thumbnail was a smiling spider in the midst of its web.

She saw me staring. She smiled and wiggled those fingers. "My story friends," she said. "You'll get to know who they are if you truly do read all these books. Or perhaps you know some of them already."

Then she took my hand. I noticed right away how warm her handshake was. "Edith Rosen, small librarian at large," she said with a sly smile. "And you?"

"Howard," I said. "Howard Camp."

She nodded and put a hand on my shoulder as she guided me toward a stack of books that she had obviously just unpacked from one of the boxes on the floor. Her long fingers gently tapped their way along the stack of books. "Stevenson," she said with a nod. She sounded like a doctor prescribing medicine. She pulled a book out of the stack and handed it to me. "You've read *Treasure Island*?"

"No," I said. "Not yet."

She took the book back from me. "I'll hold it for you. You can come and sign it out next period. Now you need to join your class on the playground. We'll see each other later."

And she was right.

THE FIGHT

I woke up because they were arguing. I must have heard them even before I was fully awake because the fight began in the dream I was having. I dreamed the world was splitting in half. There had been a nuclear bomb blast.

That autumn we had drills in school about what to do if the Russians attacked us with an atomic bomb. The war in Korea was over and our soldiers had come home, but everyone knew we weren't safe. President Eisenhower said that we had won an armistice on the battlefield but not peace in the world. There were lots of things to make us scared. I'd heard my teachers talking to one another about how the Communists had driven the French out of Indochina and how it was just the start. Our country had set off a hydrogen bomb in the Pacific Ocean that was so big it had wiped out an entire island. Now everyone was worried that the Russians would get bombs like that, too. Even nature seemed to be more dangerous than usual. Just before school started, Hurricane Carol had come roaring up the coast, killing sixty-eight people in Long Island and New England. The winds hadn't been that bad in Sparta, but we'd lost power for two days, and we still had broken trees and branches in our backyards.

In school we had to learn a song called "Duck and Cover, Duck and Cover." It was about what to do when *it* happened. We had to get under our desks. Even then I had known how dumb that was. Our desks were not concrete fallout shelters buried ten feet underground, like the one the president of the local bank had in his backyard. I knew about it because my father was one of the people the bank president had hired on weekends to help dig the hole.

In my dream, the bomb had actually fallen. I'd seen the sudden glare and then felt the shock wave, but I was still alive somehow. The only thing was that the world was broken in half. As I stood there, the two halves got farther and farther apart. I don't know where I was standing, but I could see that Mom was on one half and Daddy was on the other. They were drifting farther and farther apart into space. And they were yelling at each other. I couldn't tell what it was they were saying, but they were angry.

I opened my eyes. It was still dark outside, either very late at night or early before sunrise. The world was still in one piece, but my parents were fighting. I could hear their voices coming from the kitchen and, unlike my dream, I could understand what they were saying.

"Can't you get it through your head?" Daddy yelled. It was the first time I'd heard him raise his voice that much since Uncle Louis had stopped him from hitting me. "I ain't got a choice. You should thank God I still got a job. You know how many people are unemployed now?"

"But you're working yourself to death," my mother fired back at him. Then her voice got softer. "And don't yell," she said. "You'll wake Sonny."

"I ain't yelling," my father said, his voice was softer now, too. "I'm just telling you I got no choice. This is a recession, for cripe's sake. We need the money."

"We need you more than we need the money," my mother answered. She didn't sound angry anymore, just tired.

They both stopped talking then. I could hear them moving around in the kitchen. I knew from the sounds of it that Mom was packing up a lunch pail. I heard the front door open and close and the sound of our car starting. Then my mother came into my room. I'd already closed my eyes. She moved the glass of water off the chair by my bed and sat down. She brushed the hair back from my forehead and put her hand there. I kept very still.

"Shhh," she said in a very soft voice. "It's all right, Howard. It's all right."

She kept repeating that for a long time. But even though she kept mentioning my real name, I didn't feel like she was really talking to me.

73

That day when I got to school, I couldn't think of anything except my parents. Something between them seemed different. What was going to happen now? I felt like I was walking around underwater. I took my book back to Mrs. Rosen. She'd been right. I had loved *Treasure Island*.

"Thanks," I said, moving my mouth but not really hearing my own words. "It was great."

Mrs. Rosen took the book and held it for a moment. She could tell something was bothering me.

"I gotta get to class," I said, grateful that all Mrs. Rosen did was look at me for a minute before nodding.

I was still walking around in a fog when it came time for recess. As always, I was the last kid on the playground and the usual basketball game was being played. I hung back as always. Lately I hadn't even gotten picked to play because there were just enough boys in my class to make up two sides with six on each team. As I leaned against the side of the school, though, I realized someone was calling my name.

"Camp! Hey, Camp!"

I looked up. It was Verney Wooley. "Come on, we need another man. Take off your shirt, eh?"

Then I remembered. Tim Cote was out sick, and he was always picked for Verney's team. The teams were always shirts versus skins, with the boys on one side taking off their shirts so you could see who was on your team in a game. I hesitated. If I just walked away, I know they would ignore me. I'd be invisible again. But for some reason I didn't. I found myself taking off my shirt, my feet carrying me out onto the playground.

"Take it out," Verney said. "You can do that, can't you?"

He threw me the ball, and I caught it. I hadn't really noticed until then how much easier it was for me to catch the basketball than it had been just last spring. My hands really had grown — if not bigger, then stronger — maybe from all the man's work I'd been doing at home now that Daddy was always at the mill. I bounced the ball once and passed it back to Verney, straight and hard.

"Okay," he said, and the game began.

I'm not sure why, but the game started to mean

something to me. When the ball came to me the first time, I didn't shoot it, but I did a good job of dribbling it and not getting it stolen like usual. And when I passed it, it was right into the hands of Dwight Thomson, who was on my team and was way upcourt and made the shot.

"Two nothing, skins ahead," Verney yelled. "Winner out, eh?"

And once again he tossed the ball to me. This time I threw it to another player on our side, Dwight's twin brother, Eddie. My pass went just where I wanted it to go, right over the heads of two of the shirts.

I'm not sure if we won or not. In a schoolyard basketball game there were always arguments about what the score really was. All I know is that I *played*. My heart was in the game, and I was trying. In the past it had been easier to hide than try. I was good at hiding. I'd hidden my face at times in past years when there were finger marks on my cheek from Daddy's hard hand. But not hiding, not having to hide, made me feel so good. I even shot once at the basket. It didn't go in, but Dwight slapped me on the back and yelled, "Good try," when the ball rolled around the rim before falling out.

When recess was over, and we were pulling our shirts back over our sweaty heads, I felt somebody poke me in the side. It was Verney. He was grinning.

"Camp," he said. "you're not bad. You just need to practice your jump shot, eh?"

"Okay," I said, not sure how it had gone from being one of the worst days of my life to one of the best.

OCTOBER

MOON OF
LEAVES FALLING

NUMBER
THREE

I was taking the long way home from school the day it happened. I knew a trail that swung behind the paper plant and down by the river. I'd used that trail for years to avoid Verney Wooley and his gang, who walked on Main Street between the school and my house. But I was no longer worried about Verney. It was almost like we were becoming friends. I even met up with Tim and Verney and Dwight and Eddie on the way to school. I'd gotten more interested in sports and listened to the World Series, so we had all been talking about that. The other guys were all rooting for the Giants, but I still had my hopes on the Indians — even though the Giants ended up sweeping the series.

I still hadn't told the other kids about my secret trail. Like the trail that went to the river from our house, this one was a secret. I could swing around the park, down through the sumac trees and blackberry tangles by the railroad and back up again one side of the bridge. It was a roundabout way, but it had always made me feel safer in the past. Even though I was no longer afraid of the other kids, I still liked going my hidden way now and then. I pretended that I was an old-time Indian scout — like Uncas in *The Last of the Mohicans*.

I had asked Mrs. Rosen if she could find me a good book about Indians, not just any Indians, but the Indians who lived around here.

She had raised one long finger — the one with Black Beauty painted on the nail. "James Fenimore Cooper," she said. Then she walked her fingers along the shelf behind her, without even looking, and pulled out the book.

I was already ten chapters into the long novel. Just as

she told me, it took place right on our own river back in the Colonial times.

"Some of the language is a bit archaic," she'd said to me as I took the card out of the pocket in the back and wrote my name on it, "and Cooper does have his demerits, but I think you're ready for this."

She was right. It was hard going, but the exciting parts made it worthwhile. Like Uncas, I preferred peace, but I had learned to keep my eyes and my ears open. Ready for trouble.

I wasn't ready for the siren, though. It was the horn that went off at the paper plant at noon for lunch and at 5:00 P.M. for quitting time. But it wasn't even 4:00 yet. Then I heard another siren coming from the direction of the firehouse. I started running. There were only three reasons for the sirens going off at this time of day. The first was a fire. The second reason, which was awful, was that the Russians were attacking. The third was worse. It meant there was an accident at the mill.

I didn't run toward the sirens. I ran away from them, toward our house. I pushed my way through the brush and the briars, no longer paying attention to the trail. I just knew I had to get home. I know it made no real sense, but I kept telling myself that if I could get there soon enough, nothing would be wrong. But I didn't get there soon enough. My mother was just coming out of the door as I reached the driveway. Uncle Louis was in his truck with the motor running.

"Get in," he said to both of us. "It's Number Three."

THE HERO

My father was finally a hero. He hadn't been one in the world war, and his accident meant that he hadn't been able to go to Korea, either. Though it wasn't his fault, I think he had always felt that not being able to serve his country had made him look like he'd been afraid. He had always wanted to do something to prove that he wasn't a coward. I think that may have been why he was so brave that day in the plant. It was his chance.

Just like Daddy had told me, it was a green kid from the hills who got in trouble. They'd started hiring again at the mill, so there were a bunch of new men. Even though it was his first day at work, that kid should have known better and worn a short-sleeved shirt. His long shirtsleeve got caught in Number Three.

"Oh, my God," the green kid screamed again and again, Daddy told me. Number Three was pulling the kid in.

It was happening so fast that nobody could do anything. Nobody except Daddy. He came flying across the floor with a knife. He reached down into Number Three and cut the kid's sleeve free with one hand while he pushed the kid back to safety with the other. The kid would have been dead if Daddy hadn't done what he did.

And my father's right hand would not have got caught in the hungry mouth of Number Three.

They were loading Daddy into the ambulance when we got to the plant gate. We followed it the fifteen miles over the mountain to the Glens Falls Hospital. I wasn't crying as I sat between Uncle Louis and my mother, but she kept patting me on my shoulder.

"Big Jake is going to be all right," she kept saying. She said it so many times that it truly scared me. I couldn't remember the last time she'd called my father by that name.

When they finally let us in to see Daddy it scared me even more. He was so pale looking and his face was all scratched up. For some reason, he looked almost like a kid. I'd never seen my father look weak or small before.

"I'm all right," he said in a dry throaty voice as soon as he saw us. He tried to hold up his bandaged arm, but it was too much for him. "I yanked myself free before I got pulled in too far," he said. "I made sure they saved most of it."

My mother was frozen with her hand against her mouth. Uncle Louis picked up the paper cup by the bed and held it to my father's lips so that he could drink.

"We know that, Jake," he said.

"I guess it wasn't so hungry this time," my father said. Then he giggled like a young boy. "It only ate one of my fingers and part of another."

My mother was by his side now. Her hand was on his forehead pushing the hair back just like she did with me. It made Daddy look younger than a man with so much weight on his shoulders. For the first time I noticed that my father's hair was just like mine.

"Shhh, darlin'," she said. "Shhh."

"I deserved to lose that hand," Daddy said. "That's the same hand that I always . . ."

That was when my father started to cry.

I took hold of Uncle Louis's hand and looked up at him. He nodded at me, and we stood there together quietly while my mother took care of my father.

NOVEMBER

FREEZING MOON

A HAND

We kept waiting for the settlement check to come in. Because Daddy had been hurt on the job, he was supposed to get a lot of money.

"Enough for us to live on for a while," Daddy said. "Until I can figure out what I can do."

But the check didn't come. There was some kind of mix-up in the accounting department in the mill's main office, which was out of town. Everyone said it was coming and, for a while, Daddy's foreman tried to help. But it didn't come and it didn't come. Every time Daddy called, the people in the office at the plant just kept promising it would be straightened out. In the meantime, it was hard having Daddy home. It wasn't just the lost fingers, but the fact that so many of the bones in his hand had been broken. And his elbow and shoulder had been pulled out of joint. The first week wasn't so bad. With Daddy home it might have been almost like a holiday if he hadn't been in so much pain. Lots of the men from the mill had stopped by the hospital after their shifts to tell him what a good thing he had done, and some of them still came by the house for the first few weeks after he got back.

Daddy's foreman, who turned out to be Verney's father, visited on the first weekend Daddy was home. Verney came with him. The two of us played catch out back with a football while Mr. Wooley talked with Daddy. I learned later that he even tried to give Daddy some money out of his own pocket, but Daddy was too proud to take it, saying that the check due him from the mill would be enough, though he surely appreciated the gesture. On his way out, Mr. Wooley had shaken my hand.

"My son tells me you're not a bad ball player," he said. "Maybe we'll see the two of you on the high school team in a few years, eh?" Then he looked back at the house and nodded. "Your father's a brave man, always was a good hand. Not many'd risk their lives for someone they don't even know. I'm sure you are proud of him, eh?"

A good many wives from the mill had also stopped by our house in the first few weeks after Daddy's accident. They brought casseroles and helped Mom in the kitchen. But as the days became weeks, people stopped visiting us. Folks didn't stop talking about what a brave thing my father had done, but they had to move on with their own lives. So did we, though it wasn't easy.

⑤　⑤　⑤

Uncle Louis came by every day now. It was hunting season. If my father hadn't been hurt, he'd have been using his sick days to get his deer, like all the other men in the plant. Deer meat helped feed most of the families of the plant workers. Uncle Louis had already shot his own deer. Half of the venison had gone to our family and most of the rest Uncle Louis had given away to those others, as he said, who needed a hand. But Daddy wouldn't be able to hunt this year, even though he already had his license and his deer tag. You had to tie the tag to your deer's horns. If a warden were to see you without one, you'd get a big fine, and the deer would be confiscated. My mother gave Daddy's deer tag to Uncle Louis. That way Uncle Louis could hunt for him, even though it wasn't strictly legal.

"What is it like killing a deer?" I asked. After having watched Uncle Louis walking among the deer, I was a little troubled by the thought of him shooting one, though I had imagined Uncle Louis running through the woods like Uncas in pursuit of a deer. I'd kept reading *The Last of the Mohicans* all autumn. I was on the last pages, and I was worried about what was going to happen.

Uncle Louis put his hand on my shoulder. "It's like you take on the weight of its life, Sonny," he said. "But it is something you have to do in order to help your people survive. The deer understand that. That's why I don't chase after a deer. I just go to this ridge top I know and wait for a deer to come and give itself to me. You understand?"

"I think I do," I said. "Is that the Indian way?"

Uncle Louis looked into my eyes. Then he nodded. "Yes," he said. "That be the way to do it."

On the second week of deer season, he pulled in with a deer that had given itself to him. The deer tag tied to its horns had my father's name on it.

Daddy came out of the house to look at it. His arm was in a sling now, and it didn't hurt so much for him to walk around as long as he didn't overdo it.

"Who gave you my deer tag?" he said, frowning at Uncle Louis.

"Jake!" my mother said.

"I have to thank you, then," my father said. But there wasn't much thank-you in the tone of his voice as he turned and went back inside. My mom and I rode with Uncle Louis over to the corner store where he and I hung up the deer in the meat locker. The next day, the butcher would cut up our deer and just take part of the meat for his payment.

"He shouldn't come around so much," my father said that night to my mother as we sat down to dinner. "People will notice."

In the past when my father had given my mother what sounded like an order, she'd always agreed or at least made as if she was listening to his words. But this time was different.

"Jake," she said, "everybody in this town notices. They have been noticing for a long time. Don't you remember how they treated your family? They don't just have to look at Louis. Look at us, look at your own face in the mirror. We're not hiding anything. You should be glad that Louis is around to lend us a hand. What are you afraid of?"

"You know what I'm afraid of," he said. "The only way the boy is going to do better than we did is if he leaves all of that behind. All of it!"

I waited. This time I was finally going to find out what it was between Daddy and Uncle Louis. But it didn't work out that way. My parents looked over at me, as if just remembering I was in the room with them. Then my father just left the table and went to the bedroom. A few minutes later my mother got up and went after him with a plate of food.

Things weren't back to normal. I wondered if they ever would be. And then I wondered if they ever had been.

DECEMBER

MOON OF
LONG NIGHTS

SECRETS

Things kept on changing. The disability money was still not coming in. Daddy had taken to walking to the mill every day to check with the office. Sometimes he would end up sitting there for hours, waiting to talk to someone. They were working on it, he was told. He hadn't been forgotten, they said, but he just had to understand that a lot of paperwork went into this sort of thing. My mother took a job at the Five-and-Dime down in Saratoga fifteen miles away to make ends meet. She earned enough to pay the bills and get groceries. She was even able now and then to put a few dollars aside in the cookie jar in the kitchen.

Now when I came home from school, more often than not, neither of my parents would be there. My father was no longer able to drive the car because my mother needed it every day to get to her own job and back. But he couldn't abide just sitting around the house, and when he wasn't at the office in the mill, he took long walks along the state road by the river. He never came home before dark.

We'd had three good snowfalls and the whole town was all covered in white. It wasn't just the roots of the trees that were hidden now, but the whole of the earth. I still knew that the good brown soil was out there, though. Hard and cold as things might be now, there would always be spring when the green and growing would push up.

And the winter wasn't that bad for us kids. We made snow forts at school, had snowball fights, and there were lots of good places for sledding, including the hill right behind our house. Not only that, the winter gave me another opportunity to help out. Tim Cote's home was the closest to mine and, at school, after the first six-inch snow, he had asked me if I had a snow shovel.

"Of course I do," I said. I'd had to use that shovel to clear our driveway out to the road that morning so that Mom could get her car out to go to work. It was still too hard for Daddy to do something like that, even though he tried and finally had to stop when his face got all pale and he couldn't stand up from the pain in his arm.

"Want to make some money?" Tim asked.

So the two of us met with our shovels after school and went around from house to house where people weren't cleared out. We knocked on doors and offered our services. Fifty cents to clear a walk, a dollar to shovel out a driveway. Between the two of us we made six dollars before it got dark. I walked home with three dollars and put it all into the cookie jar before Mom or Daddy got home.

Even though my parents weren't home after school, I didn't come back to an empty house. Uncle Louis was there. It was almost as if he had moved in, leaving his little shack up in the hills where there was no running water and the only light, aside from the sun, was from a kerosene lantern. He'd taken a liking to listening to our radio, and he was usually sitting in the living room with it tuned in to one of the adventure shows. *The Green Hornet, Captain Midnight, The Shadow* . . . Uncle Louis and I loved them all — turned up loud! Our favorite was *Straight Arrow*, about an Indian who pretends to be a white man, but takes on his real identity to fight for justice. The only other Indian on the radio was the Lone Ranger's sidekick, Tonto, but Uncle Louis wasn't partial to him. He didn't like the way he talked. No real Indians talk that way, Uncle Louis told me. I was always impressed by how much Uncle Louis knew about real Indians. He seemed to have spent a good deal of time studying them.

At times, Uncle Louis was the one who had the meal cooked and waiting when my mom got back home from work after the store closed at 6:00 P.M. That's how it was on that last day of school in December. Uncle Louis's truck was in the drive, Fred Allen's show was blaring out of the radio, and the smell of pork and beans came from the kitchen.

Despite the cold, Uncle Louis was sitting on the porch waiting for me. *The Last of the Mohicans* was in his hand. As soon as he held it up I remembered. I had finally finished reading it a while ago. It was supposed to be returned to the school library the week before, but I'd forgotten about it. In part it was because the ending was so sad — with Magua killing Uncas, the best Indian of all. I had stuck the book under my bed and put my head under my pillow and cried. I imagined Uncas's father saying, *I am the last of the Mohicans.* I imagined his voice was just like Uncle Louis's.

"Miz Rosen called," he said. "She says you forgot this, and she'll be at the school for a while yet so as you can bring it in." He looked at the book in his hands. "If I was a sight better at reading, I think I might like this one. Even if the name of it ain't quite right."

"Do you know Mrs. Rosen?" I said.

"I've done talked to her a time or two down to the post office."

I tried, but it was hard to picture them together at the post office. The world of the school library was so different from Uncle Louis's. And I'd never seen Mrs. Rosen anywhere but in the library. I realized I'd thought of it as the only place she could be.

Uncle Louis stood up. "Come on," he said. "I'll keep company with you. The pork and beans won't be ready to come out for least another hour yet."

Mrs. Rosen was waiting in the library. I handed her the book with an apology on my lips.

She held up the finger that bore the image of Charlotte the spider on its nail and touched her own lips with it. "Shhh," she said. "No apology needed. It's hard for anyone to give up a book they love. Especially one that means so much to them. Isn't that so, Mr. Lester?"

Uncle Louis nodded. "I expect so," he said. "Not being much of a reader, I wouldn't know for certain. But it's true of other things."

He smiled at Mrs. Rosen, and she smiled back. It was as if the two of them were talking a language that only they knew.

Uncle Louis walked over to Mrs. Rosen's desk and

looked closely at a picture in a silver frame. I'd never noticed it before. The picture showed a well-dressed couple with serious faces, their arms around a young woman.

"Them would be your parents, then?" he said. His voice, which was always soft, was even more gentle now.

"Yes," Mrs. Rosen said. "They did not make it out of Germany. That picture was taken a month before they sent me off to England. They had to do it in secret. They would have done anything to save me. But that is just the way parents are, isn't it?"

"Sometimes people jes have to do the hardest things for their children," Uncle Louis said. I noticed his eyes had become moist.

Mrs. Rosen took his hand and patted it. "I always say that I was one of the lucky ones."

Uncle Louis nodded. "And we are lucky to have you here."

As we walked back home Uncle Louis was silent. My head was spinning. I knew Mrs. Rosen was Jewish. She had explained that to me not long after we'd met that first week in school. I had wanted to ask her about the star pin she always wore over her heart. She noticed me looking at it while I was helping her shelve some of the new books.

"Would you like to know about this, Howard?" she said.

"Yes, ma'am," I said.

"It is the Star of David," she said. "A very ancient star."

"Like David in the Bible?"

Mrs. Rosen smiled as her finger caressed the pin. "Yes, the very same. This star is a sign of my faith." Mrs. Rosen drew herself up a bit then so that, short as she was, she seemed to be standing tall. "It is a sign I have chosen to wear to let everyone know how proud I am of my Jewish ancestors. My mother gave me this pin. It is the only thing I have of hers."

But even when Mrs. Rosen told me that, I had still thought she'd been born here in America. Hearing what she said now in the library made me take a deep breath. I understood just what she meant when she said her parents didn't make it out of Germany. They had died in a Nazi concentration camp. I'd never met someone who had lost their family that way. I don't exactly know why, but I thought of Daddy. I didn't know what I'd do if I lost him.

The house was still empty when we got back. Uncle Louis checked the pork and beans. Then he came back into the living room where I was fiddling with the radio, its vacuum tubes whistling as I tried to find a station. It was a big, old, floor model, about as tall as I was. We weren't rich people, so we didn't have one of those new smaller radios, and a television was out of the question. Not with Daddy out of work. It wasn't that you had to be wealthy to own a television. Only five years ago, there had been only one television set in our whole town. Now close to half the homes in Sparta had television sets of their own. You could tell whenever another house got a television because you'd see the great big new aerial up on top of the roof. It was something to watch someone struggling up a ladder to his roof with one of those aerials, like a great big square umbrella without the cloth, then see him struggle to fasten the tall metal pole to the chimney. I had read in the *Glens Falls Post-Star* about a new kind of television set that had what they called "living color." But I didn't think it very likely that most folks would ever be rich enough to own a color television of their own. Anyway, it was a whole lot better to go down to the community theater in Saratoga to watch a movie, like *The Greatest Show on Earth* or *High Noon,* in CinemaScope on the big screen. There was no way there could ever be a movie like that on television!

Uncle Louis sat down on the couch. I turned off the radio. It seemed as if he had something to say, but I had something to ask him, too.

"Why were people like that in Germany?" I said. "Treating the Jewish people that way?"

Uncle Louis spread apart his dark leathery hands and looked down at them. "Sonny," he said, "when folks convince themselves that one particular group of people is no good, most anything can happen. And not just in Germany."

I tried to understand what he was saying, but it all seemed so wrong, so stupid. Just being Jewish didn't make people no good any more than being left-handed or having blue eyes. "I just don't know how they could do it, a whole country."

Uncle Louis looked at me and sighed. "Laws," he said. "Laws." He looked over at the front door, as if expecting to see someone there. But the door stayed closed and no one came in, even though it was about time for my mother to be getting home from work.

"Sonny," Uncle Louis said, "there is something I have got to tell you. Your friend Mrs. Rosen is right."

I looked at him in confusion. "Right about what?" I said.

Uncle Louis leaned close to me and put his left hand on my chest, right over my heart. "She is right about the fact that parents have to do hard things sometimes. Things that seem like they're best for their children. I have talked it over some with your mother, and she allowed that it was my decision. I reckon it is time that I showed you something. And I better do it now before I change my mind about it. Once you keep a secret so long, it ain't easy to let it go."

Uncle Louis pulled out his old hand-tooled leather

billfold and opened it up. From inside it he pulled out a piece of paper that was yellow with age. He unfolded it and handed it to me.

"This explains it some," he said. "Just look close at it. Take your time and don't hurry."

It was some kind of printed-out form, like you get from a doctor's office. I could tell that because of what the first lines said. Most of it had been printed up, but the names and the dates on the paper that had been filled in were all written in ink.

We, *Harmon P. Wilcox* and *Frederick Daniels Murtaugh,* physicians and surgeons legally qualified to practice in the State of Vermont, hereby certify that on the *12th* day of *March* 1932, we examined *Sophia Lester,* a resident of *Highgate,* Vermont, and decided:

(1). That She is an idiot feebleminded insane person and likely

(Strike out inappropriate words)

to procreate imbecile feebleminded insane persons if not sexually sterilized;

~~(Strike out inappropriate words)~~

(2). That the health and physical condition of such person will not be injured by the operation of vasectomy salpingectomy;

~~(Strike out inappropriate words)~~

(3). That the welfare of such person and the public welfare will be improved if such person is sterilized;

(4). That such person is *not* of sufficient intelligence to understand that She cannot beget children after such operation is performed.

Signed in duplicate this *12th* day of *March* 1932,

Harmon P. Wilcox

Frederick Daniels Murtagh

I read the whole thing through twice, trying to understand it. I looked up at Uncle Louis.

"Well?" he said. His eyes were moist.

I thought I could guess, but I had to ask. "Who was Sophia Lester?"

"That was my wife," he said. "I never called her Sophia, though. Sophie was what she preferred."

I was still struggling with what this paper meant and why it was so important, why its importance made it feel so heavy in my hands. I was confused. "What does it mean that she was . . . sterilized?" I asked.

"It means they made it so as she couldn't never have children again," he said in a voice as soft as a whisper.

The paper felt hot in my fingers. I handed it back to Uncle Louis, who took it from me without looking at it, his eyes holding mine.

"Was she feebleminded, Uncle Louis?"

"Not one bit, Sonny. Never. She was always sharp as a tack."

"Then why did the doctors say she had to be sterilized?"

Uncle Louis took a deep breath, the way I'd seen divers do before they jumped off the cliff into the deep part of the river upstream. "They done what they done because it was the law and because she was Indian. Just like me."

ROOTS

I stared at Uncle Louis. I knew what he had said, but I wasn't sure I had really heard it right. Uncle Louis was an Indian. It explained why he knew all the things he knew. The world felt like it was spinning around me. I wasn't sure if I could keep standing up. Part of me was angry because no one had ever told me. Why had everyone kept it from me? But part of me wondered if what I had heard was right. Uncle Louis said he was an *Indian*?

Uncle Louis read my mind. "You heard me right, Sonny. But there's more. Your mother always intended to tell you. She just thought you was too young yet to understand. And then there was your father always telling her to keep quiet about it. He didn't want you ever to know. He thought it would protect you."

"Protect me from what? How would my not knowing you were Indian protect me, Uncle Louis?"

Uncle Louis reached out and took my hands off the radio. I hadn't realized that I'd been rocking it back and forth until then.

"From people who'd treat you like you was less than you really was just because you was Indian. People who might even feel they had a right to do things to you, like they done to us in Vermont. That was why we left, you understand."

"Uncle Louis," I said. "I don't understand. I don't understand."

Uncle Louis took a breath and looked toward the door again. There was still no sign of my mother.

"I'm not your uncle," he said. "Your mother is my daughter. Sonny, I be your grandfather."

This time it was too much for me. I had to sit down.

"I don't understand," I said. "I don't understand." I couldn't stop saying those words.

Louis put his arm around me. His hand was gentle on my shoulder, but I could also feel the muscles of his arm against my back, muscles as hard and strong as stone or the roots of an old maple. He waited until I stopped babbling. Then, in a slow quiet voice, he began to tell the story.

"It does take some telling," he said. "To start off with, the Lesters, *your* family, we ain't French. We be Indian, Abenaki, and Mohican, mostly, though there rightly is some French in there. Some. Your father's family, the Camps, they have got a good bit of Indian in them, too. That's one reason why some of the people around here always looked down on them before your daddy come along."

Louis had taken his arm from around my shoulders so that he could place his right hand on his chest. His other hand was on my chest now, over my heart. "Your daddy," he said, "he is a good man. He'd do anything that he thought would be good for you and your mother.

Hiding your roots might make it better for you. If not being Indian might mean that people would treat you better, if it meant you'd have more of a chance in life, well, then, that was how it would be."

Louis shook his head. "But it don't work that way. No matter how hard you run, you don't never get away from your shadow. And roots is what helps a tree to stand up against the wind. Your family is always your family. That is why, even though we had to give her away, I always stayed close to your mother."

Now there were more questions filling my head, swirling around like leaves caught in a whirlwind. And the biggest word in all of those questions was why. Why did Uncle Louis — *Grampa* Louis have to give my mother away? Why had they hidden the fact that he was my grandfather?

Louis stood up suddenly and looked over my shoulder toward the door. I turned to follow his gaze. I thought at first I would see my mother. But it wasn't her. I drew in a deep breath. Daddy was standing in the doorway. The weather must have turned back to snow after we got back from the library, for there were flakes of white in his hair and on the shoulders of his red wool coat. He held something in his good hand, held it up like it was good news. It was an envelope, and I knew what it had to be. It was the settlement check from the mill. Daddy had finally gotten his money. Everything was going to be all right now.

But, from the look on his face, I could see that Daddy no longer thought things were all right. He'd been there long enough to hear at least some of what Louis had said to me — about our being Indians. I held my breath, expecting my father to look angry or begin to yell. But then I saw his eyes. There was no anger in them. Instead, he looked tired, bone tired, so tired that he seemed ready to cry. And there was a deep sorrow in his voice when he spoke.

"Oh, jeez, Louis," he said, holding out his bandaged right hand as if it was a dead bird. "Why did you have to go and do that? Why did you have to tell him? Oh, jeez!"

LAWS

My father looked at Louis and then at me. When he looked at me his face changed and I realized, perhaps for the first time, how much my father truly cared for me. The snow in his hair was melting away. But the moisture on his cheeks was not just from the snow.

Daddy shook his head and walked over to his chair, lowering himself onto it as if he were a very old man and his legs were almost too stiff to bend. He was still looking at us, at me sitting on the couch and Louis standing beside me, as straight as an ash tree. Daddy's eyes had not left us once since he came into the room. Then he sighed, and I let out the breath that I had been holding all that time.

"You might as well be hung for a dollar as for a dime," he said. "He's telling the truth, son. He's your grandfather and your family is white-trash Indian on both sides. I won't deny it anymore."

Louis hard looked at my father. "Jake," he said, "you was never trash of any sort. And I told the Henrys as much when you come around and asked to marry their little girl."

"Louis," my father said, "I never knew that."

"Well, now you know."

But I didn't. And I wanted to. And I couldn't hold out any longer. "Why?" I said. "Why, why, why did . . . ?" and then I stopped. There were so many questions, each one fighting to get ahead of the others like a herd of thirsty cows at a watering trough.

Louis and my father both turned to me. And I asked the first question that reached the water.

"Why did you have to leave Vermont?"

Louis held out his earth-brown hands and looked at them. His hands and my father's were the same color.

"In Vermont, they didn't even call us Indian. They said we was gypsies because we traveled around and didn't care to own much. Those of us who lived next to the lake, they called pirates. We hunted and trapped and traded horses and made baskets. Your grandmother Sophie, your real grandmother, she was a wonderful basket maker. Then in 1931, they passed the law. Once they got laws like that, they could do what they wanted to us."

"What kinds of laws? Did it have to do with that paper you showed me? How did you get that paper? What does it mean?" The questions came out of me so hard and fast that it made me lose my breath.

Louis understood, though. He drew in a breath deep enough for both of us. "The law," he said, "was suppose to make for better Vermonters. It give the state the right to say there was people who shouldn't be able to have no more babies. That was if they were insane or feeble-minded, like the paper said. Then they would operate on that person and make it so as they could never ever have a baby again. They took it right away from you without even telling you. It was in the papers. But we didn't know about it at first. Most of us didn't read newspapers. When they sent doctors amongst us to set up free clinics, we thought they were just being kind to us. But they wasn't. Not at all."

Louis's voice trembled. He paused and put one hand to his forehead. To my great surprise, my father stood up, walked over to Louis, and gently led him back to the couch. Louis wiped his hand slowly over his face, the way you might clear away a cobweb that you walked into unseen.

"Your grandmother Sophie, she was a good deal younger than me. We had the one living child, your mother. She was almost ten years old then. But we was still hoping on having a bigger family. Our first child — his name was Howard just like you — he died of the influenza when he was three. And your grandmother had lost another child before it was born. There just wasn't doctors or anybody around to help us except for what medicine we could do for ourselves. So when we heard the state was sending us doctors and nurses, we was happy. We wanted to be strong and healthy and so we both went to that clinic. Then, because we was who we was, gypsies or pirates or Indians or idiots or however they saw us, they done that to both of us. They just decided there was too many folks like us, and they didn't want there to be no more. When we woke up, something was wrong. They had operated so that we could never have no more children."

Louis pulled out his wallet again and took out the folded paper. "None of us was ever supposed to see this. But I knew something awful was wrong, so I went to that clinic at night when no one was around. I got in through a window, and I found a whole stack of these just piled in a tray. When I found the one with my Sophie's name on it, it made me want to die or do something to them. But I knowed that would be as wrong as what they had done. So I just took that stack of papers and left."

"How could they do that to you?" I said. My fists were clenched. "Couldn't anyone stop them?"

Louis shook his head. "It was the law. And it was too late for Sophie and me once we figured out what they had done. We got hold of a dictionary and looked up them words we didn't know. They meant that doctor had done an operation to take away our children before we ever had them. I gave those papers out to everyone whose name was on it. From then on, once our people figured out what was up, all they could do was hide. If they saw a census-taker or a truck from the health department, they would just pack up and run. Your grandmother, though, she couldn't run. She still didn't feel right. She had just got sicker and sicker after we went to that clinic. I don't know if it was the operation they done on her or if it was the shock when she found out she couldn't have no more children. She just got so weak that at the end there was nothing we could do. She died to home. We buried her next to the woods where she used to love to walk, right amongst the roots of the maple trees. Your mother and I made a little fire over her grave and, after it burned down, we left some of the things she loved to wear on the ground there next to it.

"But it wasn't over for your mother and me. They had got our names when we went into that clinic. The authorities had taken down that I had a daughter. The other thing they was doing was taking away our children. They would just come and take away whole families and put the grown-ups into institutions because they was feebleminded and then give the children out for adoption to families where you would never see them again. One day they just come and took fifteen whole families off of Monument Road, like that."

Louis closed his eyes, as if he were seeing it all again. My father put his good arm around Louis's shoulder. There were tears in Daddy's eyes now, too.

"That was when the Henrys come in, bless their hearts. I had guided for Mr. Henry back in the old days when he went hunting over in Vermont. They'd lost most of their money in the stock crash, but they was good people. Just because they wasn't Indian didn't mean they didn't have good hearts. There is good people everywhere, even when there's bad laws. There's always people who know there is older laws, laws that teach us to take care of our families and keep charity in our hearts. Knowing Mr. Henry for a generous man and his wife for a woman who always set an extra plate at the table in case some unexpected guest should come to her door, we thought they might know those older laws.

"One dark night, when no one could see us, your mother and I left Vermont. We walked through the woods because we couldn't afford any other way to travel, and we didn't want to be seen. It took us a week to get here, sleeping in the woods and in caves that I knew of along the way and drinking from the springs my own grandfather had shown me. Mr. and Mrs. Henry, they didn't even hesitate when I showed up at their door. They was glad to do as I asked them to do it. 'We shall raise her as our own,' old Mrs. Henry said. Sonny, I wish you could have knowed her. She was the kindest woman with a heart of gold. And they took me on as a hired man so as I could always be there to keep an eye on your mother. The Henrys kept our secret till the day they died. They was as good a set of parents as any child could have ever wanted."

Louis stood up and held his hand out toward my father, not like he was pointing, but with his palm facing him. My father stood up to look him in the eyes. Even though I know my father was half a head taller, it seemed as if Louis towered over him at that moment.

"Jake Camp," Louis said, his voice as deep as a drum now. "You hear me. The Henrys was always proud to have you as the husband of my daughter. Except for that anger of yours, I been proud of you, too. You hear me, Jake Camp?"

Louis's hand was touching Daddy now. With each word he spoke, his palm thumped my father's chest. "Jake Camp, you let go of that shame of yours and all that anger that has gone with it."

Daddy reached up and pressed Louis's hand against his chest with both of his own hands, pressed as hard with that broken hand as with the one that was still sound and whole.

"God as my witness, Louis, God as my witness," Daddy said.

I was standing next to them now.

"Grampa Louis," I said.

I held out my arms and my grandfather pulled me against his chest, against his old red wool shirt that smelled of cedar and wood smoke and the forest that was just as much mine as it was the forest of the Abenakis and the Mohicans, Uncas and Chingachook. My father's arms, both the good one and the injured one, were around both of us. I guess all three of us were crying some.

That was when Mom walked in the door. The air was full of the smell of burning pork and beans from the kitchen, but she paid no attention to it. She knew. And I knew. I understood that we were a family, no matter what. She dropped her packages and wrapped her own arms around the three of us. We stayed like that for a long time, swaying just as trees do that are rooted deep.

AUTHOR'S NOTE

This story has roots that stretch in a number of directions. One goes back to a conversation I had some years ago with my late friend Wolfsong, who was known and loved as a traditional Abenaki storyteller throughout the Northeast. Wolfsong was not the name he was given at birth. Like many other northern New Englanders of Native ancestry, my dear friend's last name was French-Canadian, and he was raised to not talk about the Indian part of his blood. But after beginning to learn the old stories as a grown man, Wolfsong knew that he had to acknowledge who he really was. So he changed his name and proclaimed his Abenaki ancestry at his storytelling performances. Not long after he began doing this, he received a phone call from one of his aunts.

"What have you done?" she asked him. "Now that they know who we are, they can come and get us."

They can come and get us. That might sound silly to some, but not to Abenaki people. Even during the last decades of the twentieth century, the fear still existed that being known as an Abenaki Indian might have dire consequences. One of the reasons for this was the Vermont Eugenics Project.

"Eugenics: the study of and methods for improving a species genetically." That's how the word is defined in *Webster's New Riverside Dictionary*. It can be applied to the breeding of plants and animals with characteristics that make them better for human use. But eugenics has also been applied to our own human species. In Nazi Germany, there was the belief that a master race — one that was tall, strong, blond, and blue-eyed — could be created by eliminating all substandard genetic material through sterilization. Laws were passed in Germany requiring the sterilization of people with inherited diseases like hemophilia; the mentally ill; criminals; and Jews. It was only a small step from sterilization to mass extermination.

Today, people view that period of history, which resulted in the Holocaust, with horror. But few realize that the science and practice of human eugenics was being carried out in the United States before then. Led by a Vermont zoology professor named Henry Perkins, who spent years on a project tracing "pedigrees of degeneracy," a sterilization bill was passed in Vermont in 1931. (By passing that bill, Vermont became not the first, but the thirty-first state in the United States to enact such legislation calling for the sterilization of the "feeble-minded.")

Families with "diseased germ plasm" were identified throughout the state for "voluntary sterilization." Not only such hereditary diseases as Huntington's chorea, but also alcoholism, joblessness, and petty crime were blamed on bad genes. As a result, Vermont residents targeted for sterilization were often the poor or those whose way of life did not conform to that of the majority of Vermonters. "Gypsies," a word used at the time to refer not to Romany people but to Abenaki Indians, were near the top of the list. A state summary from the 1940s claims that 212 people were sterilized, but the actual number is probably far higher. Although the Vermont law called for "voluntary sterilization," many of its victims were people who were placed in institutions and then told that they would only be released if they agreed to be sterilized.

Until research done in the 1980s by Kevin Dann, a Vermont historian, brought the Vermont Eugenics Project back into the public eye, it was almost forgotten by everyone except the Abenaki. Almost every Vermont Abenaki family has a story about the period when the sterilization law was in effect, which was from 1931 until the early 1960s. I have personally heard many such tales from such prominent contemporary Abenaki leaders as the late Chief Homer St. Francis, who told me about government people coming late at night to take away whole families. Abenaki people were afraid. Some fled. Some stopped being Indian as far as the outside world was concerned.

In 1999, Nancy L. Gallagher published a book entitled *Breeding Better Vermonters: The Eugenics Project in the Green Mountain State* (University Press of New England). In her introduction she points out that:

Most poignant of all is the plight of the Abenaki Indians, the original inhabitants of Vermont.

133

Many members of Abenaki families who were investigated by the Eugenics Survey were also incarcerated in institutions and subsequently sterilized. It was the Eugenics Survey, Abenaki leaders insist, that forced Abenaki families to conceal their identity, leave their ancestral home- land, or relinquish their language, religion, and customs. For Vermont Abenakis, eugenics was neither science nor a program of human better- ment; it was an agent of their annihilation.

My family is also one of the roots for this story. *Hidden Roots* is not autobiographical, although anyone who has read my autobiography, *Bowman's Store* (Lee & Low Books, 2001), knows that I, too, come from a family that tried to hide its Indian roots. But the character of Uncle Louis is a bit like my grandfather, Jesse Bowman (who is mentioned in this book). And my narrator, Howard "Sonny" Camp, experiences some of the things I did while in grade school during the Cold War years. The mill town of Corinth, where my uncle, Jim Smith, worked for decades for International Paper, is only 14 miles away from my home. I grew up hearing stories of that dangerous and hard work.

Like Howard, I've seen the clear mountain waters of the Hudson River stained all the colors of the rainbow as toxic chemicals were released from the mill into its flow. My friend, the late "Daddy" Dick Richards, a legendary Adirondack musician and storyteller, lost his left hand to Number Three in the Corinth Mill as a young man. (Dick, whose own Indian ancestry was Abenaki and Mohawk, then taught himself how to play fiddle and guitar with only one hand.)

I've also known, in my own family, women as strong as Howard's mother, who kept their families together, no matter what. With that said, I should add that there are no excuses for domestic abuse. The traditional Abenaki belief is that we will all eventually be repaid for our actions, good or bad. If those actions have been bad and we are fortunate, that repayment will result not just in punishment, but also in the restoration of balance. We believe that even those who have done bad can reform and become good. The mind, which twisted by anger or grief or shame, can be made straight again.

What happens to Howard's father is an illustration of that old belief.

So it might be said of this story that while the characters are fictitious, the events are all real. The tree that this story sprang from is still growing, rooted deep in these Northeastern hills.

— GREENFIELD CENTER, NEW YORK
JULY (MOON OF THUNDERS) 2003